BOUND BY YOU

A Torn Series Novella

J.M. WALKER

BOUND BY YOU

Cover and formatting: Just write. Creations
Editing: Formatting done Wright

This book is a work of fiction. Names, characters, places, and incidents either are the product of the author's imagination or are used fictitiously, and any resemblance to actual persons, living or dead, business establishments, events, or locales is entirely coincidental.
All rights reserved.
No part of this book may be reproduced, scanned, or distributed in any printed or electronic form without permission. Please do not participate in or encourage piracy of copyrighted materials in violation of the author's rights. Purchase only authorized editions.

Bound by You
New Print Edition
Copyright 2017, J.M. Walker

IBSN: 978-1-365-80695-7

J.M. WALKER

Dedication

To you.

BOUND BY YOU

Love deep.
Love hard.
Love unconditionally.

BOUND BY YOU

Warning
***Due to the graphic and adult content, this book is not suitable for a
younger reading audience***

BOUND BY YOU

One

SINCE HAVING three children, nothing has been the same. Life revolved around the little people and I wouldn't have it any other way. But I missed my husband.

Brett MacLean spent day in and day out at work. Managing our ever-growing line of night clubs took most of his time. He always made time for our kids. With Miracle being ten, she had the attitude that I grew up with. I didn't know how my father did it. Living with a snobby daughter who thought she was turning twenty was enough to drive me insane. But she was daddy's little girl, just like I was. And our sons, Eddie and Patrick were mama's boys. God I loved them more and more each day. The lives that I created with another human being was surreal since it was never meant to be.

Although I had lived with Brett and have been married to the man for over ten years, I missed him. Was it possible to be with someone and feel like you didn't know a damn thing about them? I could feel us drifting apart. I could feel our love slipping between my fingers.

"Are we okay?" I had asked him on the phone a couple of nights before.

"Of course." He paused. "Why wouldn't we be?"

I bit back a scoff and chose my next words carefully. "I'm just asking."

"Evvie," he said, his voice low and gravelly. "What's going on?"

"Nothing," I mumbled. I loved him more than life itself but lately he had become so damn oblivious. Work took over since I was now staying at home to take care of the house and our children. With all of them being in school, I could go back but he was adamant that I didn't. Brett had assistants and the such but Brett MacLean was controlling and needed his hands on everything. I was living proof of that.

"If you're sure that nothing is going on, then I have to go." His tone was clipped, short and to the point and it broke my heart.

I could feel a piece of me shatter every time that I talked to him. Was this how marriage worked? After so many years, you just lose sight of things and fall out of love?

I sighed. "Fine," I said and hung up the phone.

Since then, Brett had hardly talked to me. A kiss here. A hug there. But it was different. Something had switched, turned off between us and I couldn't figure out what it was. The spark that had brought us together was simmering into a dull heat, practically disappearing before my very eyes. The attraction was still there, but the intensity wasn't and I didn't know how to get it back.

Grumbling to myself, I continued cleaning our house while I waited until it was time to pick up the kids from school. The loud bass of the dance music pounded through the living room making my hips move of their own accord. Dancing and cleaning were one in the same in my world. I couldn't do one without the other.

When the doorbell rang suddenly, I nearly jumped out of my skin. Focused on getting the house spotless, I had forgotten that I was expecting Anna Brinson, a bombshell beauty from England, over for brunch.

Being in love with my husband before we ever got married, Anna and I had clashed in the beginning. I had trust issues when Brett had a reputation and I assumed that she was trying to steal him from me. Years later, we were now friends and we couldn't be closer. I loved her like a sister that I was never blessed with. I loved my brothers but sometimes a girl needed a little estrogen in her life.

Turning off the music, I greeted her at the door.

"Hey, Evvie." She smiled and pulled me in for a tight hug. "How are you?"

I returned the embrace and let out an aggravated sigh. "Oh, I'm just fantastic. How are you?"

She leaned back, her perfect dark brows narrowing. "What's wrong?"

"Nothing. Why would you think something's wrong?" I asked, walking past her and into the kitchen.

"Because you sighed," she said, following me. "You only sigh when you're upset about something."

Damn woman who knew me too well. "I'm fine," I muttered.

"What did Brett do?" Anna grabbed a beer from the fridge and rested her hip against the counter.

"It's not even five in the afternoon and you're having a beer?" I teased, trying to get the topic of my mood off the table.

She pointed the bottle in my direction. "I'm British, remember? Besides," she winked. "It's five o'clock somewhere."

I laughed, shaking my head.

"So, talk to me, honey," her voice softened. "What's going on?"

"That's just it. I have no idea. Since I started staying home, Brett has been working overtime. I'm concerned he's going to work himself into the ground." A heavy weight lifted off of my shoulders as the words escaped my lips. If only I could tell Brett how I had felt.

"He's definitely a hard worker. What else is going on?"

I distracted myself and pretended not to hear her question while I finished up the dishes. There was no way that I would tell her that I hadn't made love to my husband in over a week. And that I hadn't felt that connection, that undying want in months. Maybe even longer.

"Evvie?" Anna stood beside me and placed a hand gently on my arm.

I swallowed hard and shook my head. I needed to talk to Brett first. He was the type of man that would lose his shit if I told someone else our problems before going to him. But I, of course, played it off like everything was fine. That little fantasy bubble popped when he came home in a foul mood.

The door slammed shut, the tension thick and I could only imagine the deep scowl he had on his handsome face.

"Is he okay?" Anna whispered before taking a swig of her beer.

"I have no idea." I stepped out into the hallway, watching him.

He didn't looked my way as he removed his jacket and hung it up in the closet. The muscles of his strong back rippled and moved over his bones, hidden by the white dress shirt that he was wearing. But I knew without even looking, exactly what he looked like. Every freckle. Every inch. Every hard part of him. He made my mouth water in the beginning but now, he made every fiber of my very being come alive. Even though something had been off for weeks, I was still attracted to him. More so now than ever.

Brett stood in the entry way and rolled up his sleeves to his forearms. Thick veins protruded under his tanned skin. Muscles hard and inviting, holding me for so many years.

"Did you want to postpone our brunch?" Anna asked, grabbing her bag off of the table.

"No." I took a breath as he walked by us without so much as a word. "Just give me a few."

She nodded and squeezed my hand reassuringly.

I followed Brett as he made his way to his office, my heart jumping hard against my ribcage. I hadn't been nervous to talk to him since the beginning when we were just getting to know each other. When he completely consumed me with every waking breath. But now, it was like I was married to a shell of the man that I fell in love with.

I had been battling insecurities since giving birth to Miracle, our oldest. Was I fat? Did he not find me attractive anymore? Was he cheating on me? I gasped at that. I could never…I would…God, it would kill me if that were the reason why he was so closed off. These were questions that I needed to ask him but every time that I tried, the words would never leave my mouth.

"Brett?" I said finally, closing his office door behind me.

He sat in the large leather chair behind his dark wooden desk and slowly turned towards me. His blue gaze met mine, his eyes sparkling with something I hadn't seen in a while. But when he looked away, that sparkle disappeared and my stomach twisted with unease.

"Something you need, Evvie?" he asked, rubbing his strong jaw. The dark scruff had grown in some and my body vibrated with the need to feel it scratch against my skin. His tone was cold, almost bored even but his words hinted at something more. He was waiting for me to tell him what I wanted. And as much as I wanted to, I found that I couldn't.

"I…I just wanted to ask how your day was." I chewed my bottom lip. "But I see that you're busy so I'll leave you alone." I quickly left the office but not before I saw the dark shadow pass over his face.

Making my way back to the kitchen, I found Anna holding a tray of sandwiches.

"Tuna, egg salad and ham. Take your pick." She smiled.

At that point, I broke. Sobs unexpectedly shook through me and I couldn't stop them.

"Oh God. I'm so sorry." Anna placed the tray on the counter and quickly wrapped her arms around me. She didn't ask me what was wrong. She didn't push me for answers. She only held me like a friend should. Like I needed.

"He doesn't want me anymore," I blurted through my cries.

"Of course he wants you." She squeezed me tighter. "I've never seen a man want someone as bad as he wants you. He loves you."

I scoffed and stepped out of her embrace. "He doesn't touch me. He hardly talks to me anymore. If he does, it usually ends in us fighting. I feel like since we've had Patrick, we've been in a funk." I let out a heavy sigh. "I miss him. I miss him so much it hurts."

Anna's eyes saddened before she glanced over my head.

The back of my neck tingled. Slowly turning around, I swallowed hard when I met my husband's cold gaze.

"I'm going to go," Anna said. "I'll see you later."

I nodded as she slid past us.

When the door closed with a soft thump, Brett took a step towards me. "What's going on, Evvie?" His deep rumbly voice vibrated down my spine, his beautiful baby blues holding me in place. Much like they used to years before. "You don't feel comfortable talking to your husband anymore?"

"You've been busy," I croaked. "I didn't want to bother you." I lifted my chin defiantly, knowing full well he wasn't believing my bull shit strength. He had ruined me. Years ago. One smoldering look from him and I was done. Finished. And I couldn't get enough.

Brett's jaw clenched. "You're worried that you would bother me? How could you think that?"

"What do you expect me to think?" I snapped. "Every time I call you, you're short with me. You're working too damn hard. God, it's turning you into a different person." I inhaled a shaky breath. "I miss my husband."

"I'm still the same man that you married," he bit out.

"Fine." I spun on my heel and moved around the kitchen, getting things ready for supper. "You believe whatever you want, Brett." I started boiling water and went to prepare the salad when a warm body stepped up behind me.

Rough calloused fingers gently pushed the hair off my nape.

"Brett," I breathed, gripping the edge of the counter.

"Nothing has changed." His hands slid down the length of my arms.

"Everything has changed." Tears welled in my eyes. "I miss you."

"I'm right here." Soft lips traveled up the side of my neck, kissing a path in their wake.

"You're not here." I pushed out of his hold and wrapped my arms around his tight middle. Breathing in the scent of leather and man, I inhaled deep.

"Evvie." He cupped my nape.

"You're not. You're in front of me. I can see you. Touch you. But you're still not here."

"I don't know what you want from me," he said roughly.

"You!" I cried. "That's it. That's all I've ever wanted. I want you." I gripped his shirt and took another deep breath, memorizing his scent. God, I missed him.

"I've been busy." He pulled away and headed to the hallway. "I love you, Evvie. I hope you know that."

"I do," I whispered. But telling me and showing me were two very different things.

Two

"DID YOU talk to him?"

I gripped the phone tight in my hands while I stirred the pasta with the other. "Not really. I told him that I missed him and he brushed it off."

Anna sighed. "Men can be so damn dense at times."

"No kidding. I swear he thinks everything's fine." I huffed, throwing down the spoon and shut off the stove. "But it's not. I can feel it. It's like a physical ache in my chest, Anna. God, it hurts."

"I'm so sorry, Ev. I wish I could give you some advice, but clearly I would not be of any help."

I laughed. Anna and my brother, Evan, have been avoiding the fact that they love each other but were too stubborn to see it.

"Are you laughing at my expense?" she asked, a teasing lilt to her voice.

I only laughed harder. "Now, I would never do such a thing," I said, taking deep breaths.

"Yeah. Okay."

"Thank you," I said once the laughter seized.

"Anytime."

"You know, if you just talked to my brother…" I suggested.

"Not gonna happen."

"Anna."

"We had our one night years ago. I left. He got mad. We were kids. I'm too old for this shit."

I sighed. "My brother can be difficult and stubborn. I know that. I *get* that. It runs in our family. Trust me."

She gave a light laugh.

"But I if you just talk to him. It's been ten years." I rolled my eyes at that. "My poor brother probably has bluer balls than Santa Clause."

Anna choked, snorting through laughter. "Seriously?"

"What? I have kids. My adult jokes are few and far between."

"With your brothers?"

I giggled. "Yeah. Well…I got nothing."

"Listen. I love you, but your brother…he's an asshole and as long as he doesn't get his shit together, I'll never be with him." Which basically said for me to drop the subject before she went all psycho on my ass.

I changed the subject to my kids. She loved talking about them and was always interested in hearing about their day and how they were doing in school. That was one thing I loved about her. She would make a wonderful mother, if she were ever blessed with that chance. But I would stop playing Cupid and let my brother and Anna come together on their own. Maybe with an added nudge here and there.

Ann and I continued chatting for a couple more minutes before she got an incoming call from the PR Firm she worked for. Apparently her boss was a scuzbucket and called her at all hours to have her run errands for him. According to her, he was hot but a douche. And he paid well so that was why she still worked for him. If I knew my brother any, he would not like having the woman he was fawning over work for some asshole, let alone a hot one.

After feeding the kids, I put a dish out for Brett. I expected him to eat in his office like he had been doing for the past couple of nights but for some reason, tonight he didn't.

The tiny hairs on the back of my neck vibrated like they did every time he was near me. At least that part about our relationship hadn't changed. I didn't have to look to know that he was behind me. I could sense him before I saw him. I could feel him before he touched me. Not getting that caress broke my heart.

The front door slammed shut, jarring me from my thoughts. "Evvie?" my brother Everett called out.

"In here," I responded, drying my hands off on a tea towel.

"Miracle and I have a date tonight. I'm taking her to see Frozen. Again."

I laughed. He sounded so thrilled about it too. "Wanna take the boys and I'll pay?"

"No need," Evan said, coming around the corner. "Ethan and I are taking them to see an action movie."

"Not too much action." Brett said, rising from his spot at the table.

"Come on, kids. What mom and dad don't know won't hurt them." Evan laughed, helping Patrick and Eddie into their coats.

"Where's Ethan?" I asked, expecting to see him.

"He's meeting us there. Had to work late at the gym." Evan tussled Patrick's hair, smiling down at his nephew.

"Have fun and behave," I said, kissing my children's cheeks.

Patrick and Eddie looked at each other and grinned. "We always behave," Eddie said, grabbing his brother's hand. "Let's go before mama asks more questions." And they both ran out the door.

I only shook my head. They definitely were taking after their uncles. "Have fun, baby," I told Miracle when she quietly came up to us.

"Thank you," she whispered. It was so quiet I almost didn't hear her.

"Hey." I grabbed her hand. "What's wrong, sweet pea?"

She shrugged and yanked out of my grip. Not meeting my gaze once, she waited.

"Miracle."

"I'm fine," she insisted and left the house.

"I'll keep an eye on her," Everett said, pulling me in for a hug.

I nodded, thanked him and closed the door behind them. Reveling in the peace and quiet, I leaned against the door and let out a heavy sigh.

Brett was nowhere to be found. He must have gone back to his office. Figured.

Grumbling to myself, I finished cleaning up the kitchen before heading to the living room. Every time my brothers babysat the kids, I could never figure out what to do with myself. If I had a husband that wanted something to do with me, then maybe I could find ways to pass the time. Like we used to. Whatever happened, whatever switched and turned off between us, I needed to get it back before it put us into a permanent rut. Did every marriage go through this? Was it normal? I was tempted to go to Brett's office and strip, demanding that he make love to me. I knew he would. He would accept the challenge and more but it wasn't what I wanted. I wanted him to come to me. I wanted the old dominating Brett that I had fallen in love with. I wanted him to throw me up against the wall and fuck me into submission. I wanted…*him*.

That spark that was there in the beginning dwindled to a dull roar as time wore on. The only way to fuel the fire back into a raging inferno would be for him to see that there was, in fact, something wrong. I just didn't know how to make that happen.

***

A heavy arm wrapped around me, pulling me against a hard warm body. Lips cascaded down the length of my neck, hot breath scorching my skin.

In my sleep-filled daze, I rolled onto my stomach, stretching my arms out beneath my pillow.

Cool air caressed my skin when the blankets were pulled off of me.

I sighed, falling in and out of sleep.

"I know you're mad at me but you need to be patient."

I frowned, definitely awake now, I lifted my head to ask what Brett was talking about, when I was pushed face first into the mattress.

Rough hands spread my legs, opening me to him. He grunted in satisfaction, trailing fingers down my spine. "My beautiful wife."

Swallowing a gasp as he slowly inched his way into my body, I chewed my bottom lip to keep from crying out. Normally I would never get mad over Brett using me for his pleasure but since we started having our issues, he would only come to me at night. But I never stopped him. I couldn't. He was Brett fucking MacLean. A God in bed and delicious as hell.

He pulled me further under him, his balls slapping hard against me. His fingers massaged and kneaded, digging into the flesh of my rear.

A small moan escaped me and although I didn't want him to know how good he was making me feel, I couldn't help it. He was amazing. Even more so now that we were older. He knew his way around my body like an artist knew their canvas. Brett was the sculptor and I was the clay. He built and molded me into what he wanted.

"Oh God," I cried out, throwing my head back.

"Is this what you missed?" he asked, covering my mouth with his hand.

I whimpered, shaking my head.

"You didn't miss my cock fucking the shit out of your beautiful pussy? It seems like it's been awhile, *lover*," he growled, pushing into me hard.

I shoved my head from his grip and rose to all fours, pushing him back. "That's because you've been an asshole."

Brett paused, towering over me.

"Is that what you wanted to hear?" I asked, glaring at him over my shoulder. "The only time you want me is during the night. Do I disgust you, Brett? Am I fat now since giving birth to *your* children?" I pushed out of his grip and stomped to the bathroom when I was tackled from behind. Landing hard on the floor with Brett on top of me, he covered my mouth again, breathing hard against me.

"You are going to listen to me and listen good, my smart mouthed wife." He thrust back into my body, pounding into me with a desperation while his words remained calm. "I don't know what's going on in that pretty little head of yours but only you know and apparently so does Anna. Before you jump to conclusions and start accusing me of shit, why don't you get your facts straight first." His hand reached under me, brushing through my folds and started rubbing at my clit.

I cried out, covering his hand with mine and rocked my hips back and forth.

"You like that," he snarled in my ear, pumping hard and deep.

Spreading my legs wider, I helped him massage my aching nub. I squeezed my eyes shut, the burn of the orgasm hovering until Brett gave the okay for me to jump. He was in control of my body. He was in control of my ultimate undoing. No matter how many times I had tried to deny it through the years, he always had the final say.

"You're going to scream." His grip on my mouth tightened, forcing my head back. "And I'm going to fuck you into submission." He licked along my ear lobe. "Like I always do."

Holding onto his wrist, I gave in, my screams muffled by his hand.

"That's it. Louder, Evvie. Let me hear how good I make you feel. Even though I know you don't want me to."

I screamed harder, mostly in frustration with the cocky asshole that I was married to.

He chuckled and cupped the backs of my knees, spreading me wider. A heavy hand landed against the cheek of my ass, the crack reverberating right through me.

I cried out, the burn of the pain sending a warmth over my skin.

Brett did it again and again.

Smack. Smack. Smack.

Tears welled in my eyes but while he hit, he pumped harder and that only brought me faster over the edge of ecstasy.

He gripped my hair, pulling me into an upright position and wrapped a hand around my throat. "If you ever tell someone else our problems without coming to me first, I will fuck you so hard, your teeth will rattle." His grip on me tightened. "Do you understand me?" he growled in my ear.

I smirked but I didn't respond.

"Do you understand me?" he repeated slowly.

"Yes," I croaked.

"Good. Ride me hard, Evvie."

I lifted my body up and down Brett's length, slamming onto his pelvis.

"Fuck." He wrapped his hand around my throat, tilting my head to meet his mouth and kissed me hard and deep.

Leaning against him, I bent my knees and pulled his cock free from my body. I wrapped my hand around the base of him, stroking him hard. The veiny ridge of the thick muscle, jumped and twitched under my touch.

Brett groaned, kissing his way down the length of my jaw.

Cupping the heavy sac beneath him, I massaged and kneaded, pushing the tip of him through my swollen folds. My hips moved of their own accord, brushing up and down the base of him.

"Fuck me, you make me so fucking hard," he growled. He grabbed my hand that was wrapped around him, replacing it with his own.

I could never get over watching him touch himself. His big hand fit perfectly around the throbbing part of his body that had brought me so much pleasure over the years.

"Watch me come for you," he ground out, his hand moving up and down in hard fast pulls.

My breathing came out in short bursts of air as I watched Brett jerk off. Placing my feet on his knees, I slid my hand down my inner thigh before reaching my pussy.

"Hmm…" He kissed my shoulder, sinking his teeth into the soft skin. "Finger your pussy."

Pushing two fingers deep inside of my body, I stroked my clit with my other hand.

"Oh yeah. Just like that," he growled in my ear.

I grinned, pumping my fingers inside of me hard and fast. "Do you like that, Brett? Watch me come for *you*," I said, using his words.

"Fuck, I love it when you talk dirty to me." He inched a hand between my legs, guiding me, helping me reach that edge. His fingers replaced mine, thrusting inside me while I stroked my clit.

I couldn't help but watch his other hand fist his cock, milking it dry. The tip was red, waiting for him to jump off the cliff into the pleasurable high we both craved. "Come on my pussy," I breathed.

He snarled, his body shaking beneath me. White jets of liquid spurted onto my mound. My name left his lips on a deep rumbly growl. In a quick move, his hand wrapped around my throat and my head was back before I could even begin to process what was about to happen. He pushed my hand away that was between my legs and thrust two fingers into me hard.

I gasped, crying out at the abrupt intrusion.

"Keep your hands on your thighs and spread your legs, Evvie," he said, watching me.

I did as he said, writhing against his hand. "Oh God."

"Feel my fingers fuck you," he said, pushing a third into my body.

"I do," I said, panting. Feeling the usual tingle that started from my toes, I embraced the warmth. "Please, Brett."

"Open your mouth," he said, releasing me.

I parted my lips, wrapping them around his fingers, the heady scent of my arousal coating my tongue.

"Taste your pleasure." He pushed his fingers deeper into my mouth. "Remember that I'm the reason for it." He pushed me off of him and rose to his feet. "Now bend over the edge of the bed. I think my wife needs to be taught a lesson."

My body vibrated, my heart jumping hard against my rib cage. This was the man I fell in love with. This was the man that took control whenever he saw fit.

On shaky legs, I pushed to my full height and did as I was told. Leaning over the edge of the bed, I gripped the sheets tight in my hands to the point my knuckles hurt.

Brett paced back and forth behind me, his thick length was ready for me again. Proud and hard, jutting forth from between his legs. He scratched his jaw, his gaze roaming down the length of my body. He paused, a wicked grin spreading on his handsome face before he leaned over me. "Do you think I don't find you attractive anymore?" he asked, linking our fingers and gripping my hair with his other hand.

I whimpered at the rough tug. "Yes."

He slammed back into my waiting heat. "Does it feel like I find you repulsive?" He pushed into me. "You make me come and I instantly become hard again. I'm always hard for you. Does it feel like I find you unattractive?" His hips sped up, powering into me with a force that I craved.

"No!" I screamed. "No. God, no. It doesn't. Please, Brett."

"Does it feel like I don't want you?" His teeth nipped and bit at my neck, his breathing deepening. "'Cause I think my cock wants you very much."

I cried out. "Oh, Brett." I moaned.

"I think you still don't believe me." He slowly slid from my body.

"I believe you. I do. Please, Brett."

"Why? What's wrong?" he asked, brushing my sweat soaked hair off my forehead.

"I want to come."

He chuckled. "You will."

My eyes widened when I felt the tip of him run over the tight spot at my rear. It had been a long while since he took complete possession of my body but I knew that there would be no going back from this.

"I'm going to prove to you just how much your body turns me on. You are beautiful. In every single fucking way." He pushed against me, diving into the depths of my very being.

I gasped at the snug tight feeling of him taking full control of my body. "Brett."

He grunted in satisfaction. Wrapping his arms around my shoulders, he pulled out halfway. "Get ready for me to own you, Evvie."

"You already do," I said, holding onto him.

"No. This is different." He slammed all the way into me, igniting a scream to leave my lips. "I'm going to destroy you. You're going to hurt for days. Ache for more. Every time you move, you will feel me everywhere," he said between thrusts. "And I'm going to prove to you over and over for the rest of tonight, just how hot you are and how *hard* you make me."

***

I rose from my spot on the patio couch and gasped when a sharp pain shot down my back making my muscles spasm.

"What the hell's wrong with you?" Anna frowned, reaching out for my hand and helped me sit back down.

"Rough night," I said, breathing through the pain. It was the next afternoon after Brett took me hard. It had been so long, I almost forgot what he could be like. Every promise he made came true. God, I hurt. Everywhere. And I was exhausted. But it had felt so good. To be used. Consumed completely. Although we hadn't talked, Brett liked to speak through the use of his body. I knew that going in, I just forgot about it.

"Did you and Brett talk?" Anna asked, taking a swig of her beer.

I shook my head, wincing through the twinge of agony. "He did get mad that I talked to you though."

Anna rolled her eyes. "We're fucking women. We talk. It's what we do."

"He understands that but not when it comes to me." I breathed through another spasm and slowly leaned back in my seat.

"Well then he needs to talk to you, Evvie. He can't just have sex with you and expect everything to be bloody better."

I laughed. Anna was British, born and raised and had lived in America for over ten years. But when she was mad, her accent came out and it was sexy as hell. And also highly amusing.

"Are you laughing at me? Again?" she bit out, her eyes twinkling with mischief.

"Yeah. Just a tad." I sighed, running my finger around the brim of my beer. "With Brett…sex is how we communicate." I realized that now. God, I was so dumb to have forgotten.

At that point, Brett took the opportunity to round the corner and make an appearance. By the dark shadow that had crossed his face, I could only guess that he had just heard what I said.

Great. Just perfect. "Hey, Brett," I said, slowly rising to my feet.

"Anna, I think it's time for you to leave," he suggested, his voice daring her to argue.

"Fine. But you be nice. She had a rough night." She winked at me.

A smug smile formed on Brett's face. "Oh I know."

"I'm going to say goodbye to the kids first." And with that, she made her way back into the house, leaving me alone with my overbearing husband.

"Sit," he barked.

Crossing my arms under my chest, I tilted my chin. "No, hi honey, how was your day?"

He closed the distance between us and cupped my nape. "I don't suggest you start something you can't finish."

My stomach tumbled at the underlining threat. "Or else what, lover boy? You going to spank me? I already know what my body does to you."

He smacked my ass, pulling me flush against him and crashed his mouth to mine.

I gasped, opening to him and wrapped my arms around his neck. The kiss was hot, needy and it heated my skin on fire.

His tongue thrust into my mouth, owning me, taking from me exactly what he knew he would get. What he would always get. My submission.

He swallowed my moans and whimpers and tugged my head back, deepening the kiss. Brett devoured my mouth, making love to me from just a kiss. He pushed against me, moving me back until I hit the brick wall of our home. "What did I tell you?" he said, his voice deep and husky. His mouth trailed kisses down the length of my jaw before reaching my ear.

"I was just talking to my friend," I panted, grazing my hands down his chest.

Brett grabbed my wrists and pulled my arms above my head. Wrapping his fingers around them, he held me restrained. "You are testing my patience."

"Yeah, well, try being married to you," I blurted. I snapped my mouth shut when his eyes darkened.

"You are lucky that the kids are home," he growled, pulling my arms taught.

"And why's that?" I asked, ignoring the bite of the brick into my skin. "I'm only speaking the truth, Brett. I don't know what's going on with you."

"Patience," he snapped. "You need fucking patience."

"I have none!" I struggled against him but gave up when his hold on me only tightened.

"What the hell do you want from me?"

"I want you to tell me what's going on. Why are you fighting with me? Why do I only get anything from you when it's during the night? How the hell do you think that makes me feel?"

"I already proved to you how hard I get." He emphasized his point by rubbing his pelvis against my hips.

I bit back a moan and pushed out of his grip. "That doesn't mean shit." I took a breath. "Are you cheating on me?" I regretted the question as soon as it left my mouth.

He released me, taking a step back. His nostrils flared, his cheeks reddening.

I didn't know what to say. I couldn't take the question back. Any woman would wonder what the hell her husband did during the day.

Brett reached into his pocket and pulled out his phone. "Anna, you still at our place?"

My heart raced, thumping a mile a minute at the coldness of his deep voice.

"No. Don't come back. That's okay." He hung up and shoved the phone back into his pocket.

"Brett," I whispered, reaching out for him.

He grabbed my hand, roughly pulling me towards him.

I gasped at the abrupt movement, staring up at him wide eyed.

Brett didn't say anything. He just stared down at me.

For the first time ever, I was scared of my husband. Not for fear that he would hurt me. But terrified that his anger would win out and completely consume him. He was pissed. And he had every right to be. We had our trust issues in the beginning. Worked through them and now this.

He let go of me and walked back into the house, leaving me alone and trembling.

Tears burned my eyes and I slumped onto the patio chair. Sometimes my words could get away from me. This time being one of those times.

What the hell did I just do?

Three

"MAMA, ARE you and daddy fighting?"

"We just had a disagreement, baby," I told Patrick. I braced myself for the oncoming badgering of questions from Miracle but when she only stiffened beside me, I let out a sigh of relief. I tightened my arm around her and kissed her head. "I'm sorry," I whispered.

"Tell daddy that," she said softly.

My heart gave a start at that. "It's easier said than done." After I asked Brett the worst question I could possibly ask him, he had left. I couldn't find him in the house anywhere. He ended up texting that he was at his club, *The Red Love*. The place that started it all, I liked to call it. But other than that, he hadn't tried to contact me. And that was six hours ago. I glanced at Patrick and Eddie curled up in their blankets on the floor. They should really be in bed but I didn't want to be alone. And I couldn't sleep knowing that Brett was furious with me.

Keys sounded in the door making the kids jump up.

"Daddy, you're home. Mommy was worried sick." Eddie puffed out his chest. "I protected her."

Brett only smiled and ruffled his hair.

"Alright kids, time for bed." I picked Miracle up, holding her against me and carried her to her bedroom. Although she was ten, she was tiny for her age due to being born premature and she still fit perfectly in my arms. Until she got too big, I would cherish these moments. She was my first. My miracle baby. After almost losing her, I held onto times like this. A lump formed in my throat and I hugged her tight.

"Are you okay?" she asked, wiping her tiny hands down my cheeks.

I nodded and placed her gently in the bed. "Get some sleep." I headed to the doorway to turn off the light when her small voice stopped me.

"Daddy loves you. Whatever he did to make you sad, please forgive him."

I inhaled a shaky breath. "He needs to talk to me."

"Talk to him first. Maybe than he'll talk back."

My head whipped around. "You've been spending too much time at Dr. Santos'."

She giggled and rolled over. "Goodnight, mommy."

"Good night, baby." I turned off the light and shut the door.

Matteo Santos was our psychologist but now, after being with him for over ten years, he was more like a friend. A part of the family, so to speak. After Brett's childhood and nightmares, the issues with his mom, he needed someone to talk to. But maybe he just needed his wife now. God, maybe *I* was spending too much time with the doctor.

I huffed and made my way down the hall, checking in on the boys. Seeing that they were both in bed already, I kissed their cheeks, tucked them in and cleaned up the living room.

Day in and day out, I cleaned. Cooked. Took care of the home. I needed my job back. I needed out. I loved managing the clubs with Brett. It was a part of me. Not being able to was about to drive me insane or worse. It would destroy my marriage.

"Evvie," Brett called out as I walked by his office.

Bracing myself for his wrath, I slowly turned around. "Yes?"

"Come here."

The short command did something funny to my belly. It twisted and turned with delight, reminiscing about the man that used to have me drop to my knees from just a word. "Brett, I'm—"

"Shut up," he snapped.

I jumped, chewing my bottom lip.

He rose to his feet and slowly made his way towards me. His demeanor was cool, collected, like it had always been but it was laced with something else.

My gaze travelled down the length of his body. The top three buttons of his white dress shirt were undone. The thickness between his legs hidden by the fabric of his black pants. My mouth watered at the mere sight of him. No matter how many times I had been with the man, it was always different. Powerful and passionate, dominating and seductive.

I was frozen in place, captivated by his stare. "I'm surprised that you came back."

His jaw clenched. Leaning his hands on either side of my head against the door, he leaned down, brushing his nose along the side of my neck. "Do you remember the issues we had in the beginning because you didn't trust me?"

"I trusted you."

"No!" He slapped a hand against the door. "You didn't."

"I did!" I cried. "I didn't trust the other women."

"And now here we are, over ten years later and you still don't trust me," he said, his voice panged.

"I hardly hear from you during the day. You're never around. You don't talk to me, Brett. You hit my brother in the beginning remember? You were jealous of my damn brothers! If the roles were reversed, you would react the same way."

"No, I wouldn't." Brett cupped my throat, tilting my head. "You want to know why? Because I trust *you*." Spinning me, he pushed me against the door and leaned into me.

"I'm sorry. I trust you. I do. I...I..."

"Do you know how hard it was for me to control myself earlier? When you asked me if I was cheating on you, I wanted to hurt you."

I whimpered. "I'm sorry," I whispered.

"Are you really?" His arm wrapped around me, holding my hands tight against my chest.

"Yes. Of course I am. I just blurted it out."

"And that's an excuse, Evvie? I would fucking die for you."

A sob escaped me. "Brett, please. I'm sorry."

"I would die for you," he repeated. "I love you. I love you more than a human should love another person. It's a dangerous love because I know that if something happened to you, a part of me would die with you. I'm sorry that you're having issues trusting me but I need you to be patient. Please." The sweet vulnerable side of him didn't last long when the force of his rage took over. Not that I ever expected it too.

"What's going on with us?"

"You tell me, Evvie. You seem to be the one with the problem." Brett released me and headed back behind his desk.

I shook myself, momentarily surprised that he let me go. I was waiting for his wrath. For him to prove to me again just how much he in fact owned me. To remind me that he was mine.

"I miss you," I said softly.

"Well I'm right here, now aren't I?" He scrubbed a hand down his face, eventually meeting my gaze.

My heart hurt. My body ached from the night before. He may have been sitting a few feet away from me, but he shut me out. He was closed off, falling into himself. "Have you seen Dr. Santos?"

Brett raised an eyebrow. "If you think whatever this shit is has something to do with my past, you need to fucking think again, Evvie."

"I just worry. Have you been having nightmares?" I walked up to him and slid between him and his desk. I was grasping at straws but I was determined to fix whatever this issue between us was.

"Evvie," he muttered.

Crawling onto his lap, I cupped his cheeks. "Talk to me."

"I'm fine. I haven't had a nightmare in years." He said those words and I wanted to believe him but when he didn't look at me, I knew he was lying.

"When was the last nightmare?" I asked, unbuttoning his shirt.

"Last night and every night before that," he ground out. "They started happening again when we started fighting."

A heavy feeling settled in the pit of my stomach and all I could do was sit there. Like a fool, I thought this shit was only affecting me. I waited for him to make a move. To hold me. To tell me that everything would be alright but when he didn't, I rose from his lap and swallowed past the hard lump in my throat.

"I don't know what's going on between us," Brett said, grabbing my hand. "But I can reassure you that I am not fucking cheating on you."

I nodded and attempted to pull from his grip when his fingers tightened around my wrist.

"I'm not." In a quick move, he twisted my arm behind my back and bent me over the edge of his desk.

I gasped, gripping the hard wooden top.

"That question hurt me, Evvie, but it pissed me off even more." His tone took on a bite, like the sharp blade of a knife.

"I'm sorry. I know you're not cheating on me," I cried out.

"Then why did you ask?" he snapped, shoving my dress to my hips.

"Because it was the only way to get a reaction from you!" I snapped my mouth shut, realization dawning on me at my outburst.

Brett paused in his movements, his hold on my wrist loosening.

"You've been cold. Closed off. And I've tried talking to you but I couldn't get—"

"Enough!"

"But we need to talk." I cried out when a heavy swat landed on my ass. The pain simmered to a dull roar but I found myself craving more. I didn't know what was going on between us. I didn't know how to even get *us* back.

"We can talk later. Right now, I'll give you the reaction that you so desperately have been trying to get from me." The sound of a belt being pulled from the straps, snapped into the air like that of a whip.

I squeezed my eyes shut, waiting for the inevitable pain that I knew would soon surround my very being.

Brett released my wrist and grazed his hand down the small of my back. In a smooth move, he ripped off my panties, pulling them free from my trembling body. "This is for thinking that I'm cheating on you."

A hard snap landed against my flesh. I cried out, my eyes brimming over instantly from the burn.

"This is for not talking to *me* but telling everyone else our problems instead."

Snap. Snap.

I breathed through the pain like so many times before. Brett and I had embraced our kinky side years ago. It was a journey that brought us closer. Built on trust and communication. But now, I just needed to feel him truly dominate me.

Sweat coated my brow, my hands hurting from gripping the edge of the desk until my knuckles turned white. "Brett," I breathed.

He stopped what he was doing and dropped the belt, landing a hard swat on my ass with the palm of his hand. "Nice and red, my beautiful wife," he purred, caressing the burning skin of my rear. His finger inched to my opening before entering my body in one smooth thrust.

I moaned, rocking back against his hand.

"Nice and wet, too," Brett said, kissing my tail bone.

I gasped when something warm and velvety ran over my center and back up between my ass cheeks. When it focused on the tight area that Brett had ripped into the night before, I couldn't help the flush of heat that spread over my body.

It was tender, loving, like he was apologizing for hurting me even though he enjoyed whenever I was sore from his rough caress.

"So fucking delicious." He snarled, licking his way into my body.

Suddenly, a sharp pain exploded through my clit. My breath caught, my heart pounding hard against my rib cage. "Oh…oh God. Brett!"

The pain only turned into a powerful force. The sweet agony mixing with pleasure.

At that point, Brett thrust into me. "*Fuck*," he groaned.

I bit my bottom lip to keep from screaming out, for fear of waking the kids.

His fingers dug into the flesh of my hips, no doubt bruising my skin. He pumped hard and fast, bringing us both over the edge of ecstasy. We jumped that cliff together, diving into the fiery pits of passion and seduction as he used my body to please him.

Brett pushed into me, going as deep as my body would allow. "You're nice and tight, Evvie. So slick and swollen for my dick. Your body loves the fucking that I give it."

I moaned in agreement. Did it ever. I could never resist the temptation of his rough touch. The way he moved inside of me like he couldn't get enough. The way he consumed my every waking breath. Every thought. Every action. Every word was for him. This shit we had going on, it wasn't important enough to throw what we had away. That. Right there. Him taking from me what he needed, what he had always needed, my everything. Every single inch of me. My heart. My soul. My mind. It *all* belonged to him.

"Come for me," he breathed heavily in my ear. "I need your orgasm. Come all over my dick, lover."

The twinge of pain spread once again through my aching clit. I didn't know what was causing the sting but the slight agony burst forth, causing a release to shatter through me. It was so hard, my vision faded in and out. I stayed still, not even screaming. The intensity of the orgasm stole my breath only causing Brett to pump that much harder inside of me.

Suddenly my body felt like it was falling. My eyes grew heavy, my limbs and muscles being pulled forth to the ground. I continued into the abyss, the darkness of my mind swallowing me up like that of a black hole.

The last thing that I heard was my husband yelling.

Four

I WOKE sometime later, curled up on the chaise in our living room, with my body wrapped around Brett.

"She's awake."

I jumped at the deep slightly accented voice and found Matteo Santos sitting on the couch.

He rose to his feet and knelt beside us. "How are you feeling, Evvie?"

I glanced at Brett.

His brow was furrowed, his strong jaw clenching and unclenching.

"What…" I cleared my throat. "What happened?"

Brett cupped my nape, rubbing his thumb back and forth over my pulse point.

"Brett?" I sat up, snuggling into his side when my body became really heavy and tired all of a sudden. Stifling a yawn, I leaned my head on his chest. "Matteo, why are you here?"

His gaze slid to Brett's before meeting mine. "Brett called me."

My eyes widened. "Really? Why? What's going on?"

"Have you heard of subspace?" Matteo asked me gently.

"Yes." I had learned about it from Brett long ago and enjoyed experiencing it every chance I could. It was different for everyone but most said you felt like you were floating. And I had to agree.

"Okay. Do you know what sub drop is?"

I felt Brett shift beneath me.

He rubbed his jaw. "She shouldn't since I've never told her," he bit out.

"No. I don't know what it means," I told Matteo.

"It can come in many different forms. Basically it's the effects of the release and drop of endorphins. It can be due to an emotional and physical response. In this case, you dropped. Hard." A shadow passed over Matteo's face, his dark eyes going cold.

"So what does that mean exactly?" I asked, ignoring the shift in the air.

"It means that if Brett wouldn't have caught it in time, you could have fallen into a heavy depression that sometimes lasts for days, even weeks." He rose to his feet, pacing back and forth before stopping at the bay window. The moonlight cast an eerie glow around the doctor, giving my heart a start.

"I'm sorry," Brett said, cupping my cheek. He placed a soft kiss on my mouth. "I...I couldn't control myself."

"I'm fine," I reassured him. "I still don't know what you both are talking about."

"You may be fine now but the point is that Brett needs to learn control. I understand that you have been having problems." Matteo turned to us. "But the pain that Brett has given you mixed with the intense pleasure, brought you over the edge into a dark place. I've seen people take weeks to get out of it." His eyes took on a faraway look.

"Oh...well, I'm fine," I repeated. I sat forward, resting my head in my hands when a pounding headache hit me full force.

"Headache?"

I looked at Matteo. "Yeah. How did you know?"

"Because my..." he cleared his throat. "I know someone that gets them all of the time while..." His cheeks reddened.

A slow grin spread on my face. "Why Dr. Santos? Do you have a girlfriend?"

"Evvie," Brett scolded.

Matteo chuckled, brushing his hand through his hair. "Curiosity got the submissive spanked, dear Evvie."

I laughed, leaning back into Brett's side.

He pulled me into his arms, running his nose up and down the length of my neck. Inhaling. Scenting me. It had been so long, I had almost forgotten what it had felt like.

"Now that we know you are okay, I will leave you alone. Brett, make sure you give your wife a safeword. Next time we meet and I hear that you haven't yet, I'll kick your ass." And with that Matteo left, shutting the door behind him.

"I wonder what the woman will be like that captures his heart," I said softly.

"Strong."

Wrapping my arm around Brett's shoulders, I kissed his cheek. "I agree."

"We can decide on a safeword later. Right now, I need to know…are we okay, Evvie?" he asked, casually sliding his hand up and down my thigh. "I mean, okay. Like before."

I pulled out of his hold and rose from the chaise. Pacing back and forth, much like Matteo had done minutes before, I couldn't meet my husband's stare. "I have loved you with all of me for over ten years. I've given you pieces of myself that I never even knew existed before meeting you." I stopped in my tracks and met his heated stare. "But something is off. I need out. Out of this house. Out of being a mother. Just for a little bit. I love my life. I love you. I love our children. I couldn't be more blessed. But I need…I feel trapped, Brett. I can't go on like this. I feel worthless. I feel like I'm not doing anything. I cook, clean, take care of the kids, take care of your needs and by the time that's all done, I'm exhausted. I'm tired." I inhaled a shaky breath.

Brett came up to me and grabbed my hands, kissing each of my fingers.

A lonely tear rolled down my cheek but I continued. "I miss you. I know you say that you are here but I don't see you during the day. I just worry that you're working too hard. That's all. It's not me being jealous or controlling. I'm not wondering if you're cheating. But I do wonder what you are doing. I just want my husband back. You used to work nine to five and that was it. But now sometimes I don't feel you beside me until three, four in the morning."

"I'm sorry." He pulled me into his arms, holding me, pouring his love for me into that touch.

"If you can't tell me what's going on or why you feel the need to work so hard, I need to leave."

"What? Like fuck you do. You need to leave," he scoffed. "I don't fucking think so," he said, raising his voice and grabbed my hand.

"I…I need a break. I need something. You can't make me stay here inside of the home. We're in the wrong era for that, Brett. I refuse to be barefoot and pregnant, cooking and cleaning just for you to go to work and come home miserable."

"Well guess what, Evvie? You can't get pregnant anymore so you won't be barefoot and pregnant."

My mouth fell, shock tearing through me at his words. "Fuck you. I only got fixed because if I had another one of *your* children, it would kill me." That's what the doctors had told us. Why he was throwing that in my face was beyond me. Either way, it was a dick move on his part.

"Shit." He scrubbed a hand down his face. "I shouldn't have said that."

"No, you shouldn't have." I went to walk by him when he grabbed my hand.

"I'm sorry." He wrapped his arms around me. "Please. You can't leave."

"Then tell me what's going on. Why are you working so hard? You're losing weight. You're miserable."

"I'm happiest when I'm inside of you," he snapped.

"But it shouldn't be like that," I cried. "You have children. Tell me what's going on. Please," I pleaded.

His breath hitched. "I can't. You need to be patient. You have to."

"No, I don't!" I shouted.

"Evvie."

"Fine. Then let me work outside of the home. Even part-time." I lifted my chin defiantly, waiting.

"I want you here—"

"Brett, please!" I shoved out of his grip. "I can't keep doing this."

"Evvie." He reached for me when I swayed on my feet. "Let's take you to bed."

"No! I don't want to go to bed. I-I want…I want…" My breathing was hard, coming out of me in fast pulls. I couldn't control my next actions. It was like I was having an out-of-body experience, looking down on myself. A frustrated woman. A woman who has had enough. A woman who was sick of seeing her husband disappear before her eyes. It was the final moment.

The next thing I knew, I was in his arms, crashing us both to the chaise. I gripped Brett's shirt, ripping it down the middle with my bare hands.

He growled, inching his hand in my hair and pulled my head back. Licking his way between my lips, he deepened the kiss. It was a calling of our love. Begging for it to resurface and wrap around us like it had over the years.

We should be talking. We should be discussing what was wrong. But Brett and I never talked. It always ended up with sex. It was the way that we communicated and I wouldn't change it for anything.

Brett reached under my dress, pushing the fabric to my hips and cupped my ass.

I moaned into his mouth, quickly undoing his belt buckle. My hands were shaky. All I could focus on at that moment was getting him back inside of me. I needed him so much it hurt.

He sat up, spinning us around the edge of the chaise and ripped open his pants.

Rising to my knees, I lowered myself onto him, his name leaving my lips on a breathless gasp.

"You should be resting," he growled. "It's not safe..." He shivered. "*Fuck.*"

"I don't care," I said, my hips picking up speed.

"Shit. I can't resist your tight body." He guided my hips, helping me ride him in slow circles. "Is this what you wanted?" he asked against the crook of my neck.

"Yes," I said, running my fingers through the hair at his nape.

"Why, Evvie? Tell me why you were so desperate to get me back inside your body," he demanded, his voice lowering.

I met his gaze. Brushing my thumb over his bottom lip, I stared intently into his blue eyes while I continued to undulate against him. "Because I realized it's how we communicate."

"You just realized this?" he asked, trailing light pecks over my collarbone.

"Well no, but I realized it more these past couple of days." Throwing my head back, I could never get over how perfect he felt inside of me. Even after all of these years.

His hips stopped, his arms wrapping around my middle, pulling me tight against him.

I gasped as he bottomed out deep in my pussy.

A wicked grin spread on his face. "I talk to you through my body because I know it's the only way you'll listen. You're submissive to me and my touch. I can get you to do anything that I want while I have you wrapped around me." He lifted me in his arms and carried me down the hall.

Crashing my lips to his, I pushed my way inside his mouth. Stroking along his tongue, I marked, claimed, reminding him that he was mine. "Then talk to me," I said against his lips. "For the rest of the night."

***

"Miracle, what's wrong, baby girl?" Brett asked our daughter a couple of nights later.

"Nothing," she said softly, pushing the food around on her plate with her fork. She had her head against her hand and sighed every so often.

I frowned, wondering what was going on but I didn't press. Not yet. I didn't want to be one of those parents that expected their child to tell them everything but it was hard. So damn hard. I knew she was hurting but I didn't know why. My motherly wrath boiled inside of me, wanting to destroy whomever wronged my baby girl.

Every now and again, Brett and I would pass knowing glances. His eyes would heat. I would grin. And I probably blushed as well. I could tell from the tingle in my cheeks. These past couple of days had been amazing. Brett wasn't working so much. He joined us for supper and I went to bed with my husband. We had spent so much time reconnecting, that my body hurt. Even *he* was walking around slowly. But we never complained.

When the phone rang, Brett answered it, winking at me.

I giggled. God, I was turning into a school girl. Never would I have thought that he could still get this reaction from me all these years later.

"Hey," Brett greeted the caller. "Yeah, she's good. We're having supper. No, she doesn't know yet."

I raised an eyebrow. "Know what?"

He chuckled. "Tonight. I think she'll like it."

"Like what?" I asked, my curiosity piqued.

"Nope. The kids haven't said anything." He laughed making my heart skip a beat. His deep vibrato washed over me sending a layer of goose bumps over my skin. He caught my look and cleared his throat. "Thank you, Matteo. For everything." He said goodbye and disconnected the call, placing his cell back in his pocket.

"So…"

"So…what?" he said, crossing his arms under his chest.

"What's going on?" I huffed.

A wicked grin spread on his face. "Why don't you come here and find out?"

God, he was so not fair. His sexual advances these past couple of days would put a porn star to shame. Even when the kids were around, an innuendo would slip, I would blush and he would laugh. Luckily, they didn't know what he was talking about. Yet.

I rose to my feet and made my way to him. "Are you going to tell me what that was about?" I asked, sitting on his lap.

He kissed my arm, placing a soft bite on the pale skin and wrapped his arms around my middle. "No."

"Brett," I cried. "You can't talk to Matteo about it, get me all excited and then not tell me." I hated surprises.

"How do you know we were talking about you?" he asked, a teasing lilt to his voice.

"Because…because…" I pouted.

He laughed and pinched my chin, placing a soft peck on my mouth. "How badly to you want your surprise?"

"Very badly," I said against his lips.

"So bad that you'd be willing to do anything to get your surprise?" he asked, lowering his voice so that only I could hear him.

My breath hitched. I didn't know what more I could possibly do that we hadn't done already. He already took me to new heights, made me aware of the things that I liked that I never even knew existed before meeting him. "Yes," I said, anyway.

A smug grin spread on his face. "Good girl."

My stomach flipped at his praise.

"Do you think mama's ready for her surprise?" he asked the kids.

Patrick and Eddie yelled *yes* but Miracle only remained silent, still playing with her food.

"Baby, what's wrong?" I asked her, taking her small hand in mine.

"Are you guys getting a divorce?" Tears welled in her eyes, her bottom lip quivering.

"No!" I slid from Brett's lap and picked her up, sitting back down in her chair. "Mama and daddy had some problems that we had to work through but we're fine now." I hugged her to me, rubbing her back in small smooth circles.

She sat back, wiping under her eyes and glanced between Brett and I. "Are you sure?"

"Of course." Brett moved his chair closer and motioned for the boys to join us. "Your mom and I have difficulty talking sometimes," he said, placing Patrick and Eddie on his knees. "But I promise you, we are not getting a divorce."

"But we heard screaming," Miracle said, her voice shaky.

My eyes widened.

Brett choked. He threw his head back and laughed.

"I was screaming because your daddy can be a meanie head," I said, glaring at him for making me come up with some random excuse that wouldn't scar our children for the rest of their lives.

He only laughed harder, his big body shaking.

Seriously. Douche.

"Are you sure?" she cupped my cheeks. "You sounded like you were in pain."

Oh dear God. That was it. My child would be ruined forever. "I'm fine," I croaked out. "I promise. No more screaming."

That shut Brett up. He raised an eyebrow, challenging me.

I only rolled my eyes and continued reassuring our daughter that we were fine. I wasn't screaming because Brett was hurting me. But I also would never tell her that I had asked for it. Shit, what kind of parent was I?

"Kids, go get your coats," Brett said, keeping his gaze locked with mine. "I think it's time we show mama her surprise."

They did as they were told, their shouts of joy filling the room.

"So, no more screaming?" Brett teased, pulling my chair towards him.

"Not if it means scarring our children and forcing them to end up seeing Dr. Santos as well," I said, crossing my arms under my chest.

He chuckled, pushing his way between my legs. "Well we do have a basement that has a lot of empty rooms. We could turn part of it into our own play room. Sound proof the walls and everything. We'll even put locks on the doors. What do you think?"

I thought a moment. To have our own room. Just for him and I. "How would we shop for that stuff?"

A slow grin spread on his face. "Well I think Matteo could help us with that."

"Seriously?"

"Lover, you do realize what he's into right?" he asked, pulling me onto his lap.

"Not really. I know he's dominating and all that stuff but…" I shrugged.

"He was born in a brothel. He probably has one hell of a story to tell."

I shivered. "Oh yeah."

"So what do you say? You want our own play room?"

"Yes." I smiled. "I want a room that's just for you and I. A room where I don't have to worry about the kids walking in." I leaned down to his ear. "A room where I can scream as loud as I want, letting you know how good you make me feel."

"Hmm." He cupped my nape, holding me in place. "I already know how good I make you feel. I know that you get wet from just my words. And I know that your pretty cunt is dripping for me right now. If we were alone, I would bend you over this table, shove my cock deep inside of your aching body until you begged me for more. Always more. You're greedy for me."

"I crave you," I breathed.

A smug smirk spread on his full lips. "I know. Now let's go before I take you to our bedroom and do dirty things to your hot body."

Holy hell. "You already have," I reminded him, thoughts going back to that morning.

He kissed my forehead. "You haven't seen anything yet, lover." He stood up behind me and wrapped his arm around my waist, brushing his mouth along the shell of my ear. "Just wait until we get our play room. I'm going to restrain you. Bound you. Spread you open so wide, your pussy will weep with pleasure. I'm going to have you writhing, begging, demanding for me to fill you with my cock. One thrust and you'll explode."

"Oh God, Brett, stop. Just stop." I shook myself, stepping out of his hold and scrubbed a hand down my face.

He chuckled, lightly swatting my rear. "Don't get used to those words, Evvie, because *stop* is not a safeword."

Five

"KEEP YOUR eyes closed, mama," Eddie said.

I could feel him bouncing in his seat beside me. I laughed, my hands covering my eyes. Brett had rented a town car to drive us to wherever it was that we needed to go. I had no idea what my surprise could be but it was starting to drive me insane. I was ready to find out. Now.

"Are you ready, my beautiful wife?" Brett asked me, his deep voice caressing my ear.

"Yes. You didn't marry a patient person you know," I grumbled.

He laughed. When the car came to a complete stop, he grabbed my wrists, pulling my hands from my face.

My eyes fluttered open, landing on the man that I had fallen in love with so many years before.

The door to the vehicle opened. "Alright, kids."

I frowned. "Evan? What are you doing here?"

He winked. "Let's give mama and daddy a moment."

"Look at me," Brett commanded softly when we were finally alone. "I love you. I love you more than anything in this whole world. You have taught me to be a better man. You have shown me that there is more to life than just money," he smirked. "And sex."

I giggled, shaking my head.

"You've given me a family, three beautiful children that mean more to me than life itself. You've given me you, my sweet Evvie."

Tears welled in my eyes.

He cupped my cheeks, placing a soft but passionate kiss on my lips. "I love you. Are you ready for your surprise?"

All I could do was nod as a lump formed in my throat.

Brett grabbed my hand, helping me from the vehicle and stood in front of me. "Before I reveal my surprise, I just want to say that I am sorry. For how I've acted these past couple of months. For being an asshole. For making you think that I cheated on you. This has all been for you but I never wanted it to go as far as it did."

"I'm just being insecure. I thought you were mad at me or that I did something wrong."

"Never," he kissed my forehead. "You could never do anything wrong."

"How are the nightmares?"

"Better." He kissed my nose and slowly turned me in his arms. "Look up."

I glanced up, my eyes widening when they landed on a large red neon sign. My name, Evvie, flashed down at me in beautiful script. "What…" My words trailed off. I couldn't believe what I was seeing.

"This is all yours, lover."

"What do you mean?" This was mine?

My brothers and my children came out of the brick building, laughing and smiling as they made their way towards us.

"Do you like your surprise?" Ethan asked, placing Patrick on his shoulders.

"I…" I shook my head. "I still don't quite understand what my surprise is."

Brett chuckled, wrapping his arms around my waist. "You told me you wanted to work again. You wanted out of the house. You needed a break. This is why I have told you to stay home. I didn't want my surprise ruined. This, my beautiful wife, is your very own club. *Evvie's* belongs to you and only you. Your name is on the lease. Your name is on the menus. Your pictures are on the walls. This, it's you."

"How…I…what…"

"I think she's shocked," Evan said with a laugh.

"Wait until she sees the inside." Everett smiled, holding Miracle's hand. "Let's go inside so mama can see what daddy has been doing for her all of these months."

"What is he talking about?" I asked Brett.

"You'll see." He slid his fingers between mine.

I couldn't imagine what more he had in store for me. My own club. *Evvie's*. I could finally go back to work after all of this time. Patrick was almost six. Six long years that I had been a stay at home mom. I was blessed that we could afford for me to do that but I was going stir crazy.

When we headed into the club, I stopped abruptly. My eyes had to have been playing tricks on me because I could swear that we were entering, *The Red Love*. Brett's club. The place we met. The place where we first kissed. Black and white pictures lined the walls in the narrow hallway. Dim lighting adorned the area before us, red carpeting lined the floor. "Brett," I said in awe.

"Let's take a trip down memory lane, lover." He released my hand and stepped in front of me, walking backwards. "You see these pictures? They are the exact same ones that are in my club. But these ones are the originals."

"How long have you been planning this?" I asked, my eyes glancing back and forth between him and the images of me. You could never see my face in the pictures. Only parts of me. My hand. My thigh. But my favorite was Brett's strong hand wrapped around my throat in a possessive but loving way.

"I've been planning this since I first started taking pictures of you." He winked. "So a long time. Can you believe our anniversary is coming up?"

"Wait." I clapped a hand over my mouth. "Our anniversary."

He threw his head back and laughed. "You forgot."

"No. I just..." My cheeks heated. "Okay, yeah. I forgot a little bit."

"It's okay." His gaze heated. "I've been distracting you."

"That is no excuse. Usually it's the man that forgets." I stepped into his arms, wrapping mine around him. "Thank you. I'm so sorry."

"There's more, but you're welcome."

"More?" I asked, pulling back. "How can there be more? Look at what you've done for me already. I could never ask for more. This...this is amazing."

He kissed me softly on the lips. "We only made it into the hallway. Let's go into the actual club."

As we walked into the club, my eyes welled. I couldn't help it. It was the exact replica of Brett's club, the only difference being that my name was on everything.

"I wanted to give you something from just me. I've offered for you to be a part in owning *The Red Love* but you, being the amazing woman that you are, said no. You said that it's mine. You said that it's the only thing that I own. Well I own you, Evvie. But this..." He swept his hand out in front of him, indicating the space before us. "This is all yours. Only *you* own this. This is my gift to you. Happy Anniversary, Mrs. MacLean."

A sob escaped me and I threw myself into his arms. No words. No words at all could describe how happy I was. To know that we were fine. That after all of these months of long sleepless nights, it was because of this. He had been planning for years this huge surprise.

He chuckled, returning my embrace. "I love you. You have done so much for me. You stuck by me when you should have run away screaming. You are the most selfless person that I know. You're an amazing wife and an even better mother. You've give me the greatest gift a man could have."

"I didn't get you anything for our anniversary," I said through my tears.

He cupped my cheeks, brushing his thumbs under my eyes. "You've given me happiness. You made me see that just because *I* had a shitty childhood, it didn't have to be that way for my children. *Our* children. You also remind me every single day that I am not a monster. You help me through my nightmares. *You* are my gift. I don't say that enough." Brett lowered to one knee, holding my hands in his. "I never gave you a proper proposal."

I laughed. I could see out of the corner of my eye that my brothers and kids were surrounding us but all I could focus on was the man staring at me from bended knee. The love poured off of him in waves, crashing into me like that of an ocean.

"I love you, Evvie. I thank God every damn day for giving me you. Will you do me the honor of spending the rest of your life with me?" He pulled out a velvet box from inside his jacket and opened it.

I gasped. A gold chain glittered up at me with a diamond pendant resting in the middle. In intimate script, an *E* wrapped around the letter *B* in a seductive way. "Oh...my..."

He took the necklace out of the box and rose to his feet. "I want to renew our vows. Right here."

All I could do was nod as he pulled the chain out and wrapped it around my neck. The pendant rested between my breasts. "Yes. I will. I will spend the rest of my life with you and longer. I will renew my vows with you every damn year."

A grin spread on his face. He picked the pendant up that sat nicely against my chest and kissed the pendant. "Brett and Evvie. Together. In more ways than ever could be written."

"God, I love you. So much. You're my life."

"My one."

I smiled. "My only."

He crashed his lips to mine, picking me up and spinning me in his arms.

I giggled, holding onto him as tight as I could.

"Mama. Mama."

I laughed and knelt, pulling Patrick into my arms, motioning for Eddie and Miracle to join in our little huddle. "My children. My precious babies. Thank you. For everything."

"Why are you crying, mama?" Patrick asked, kissing my tears away.

That gentle touch only made me cry harder. "You are so like your daddy. All of you are. I love you. So so much."

"Good job, little dude. You made her cry again," Evan teased, ruffling his nephew's hair.

"So do I get a hug or what?"

My eyes widened and I turned to the deep voice. "Kane."

He smiled and held out his arms.

I ran into them, wrapping myself around his large body. I hugged my best friend of years, with all of me.

"Evvie, you're going to hug me to death." He laughed. "Has it been that long?"

"Yes," I punched him in the arm playfully. "Way too long. How's Tatiana? How's the new place? God, I miss you both."

He chuckled lightly, rubbing a hand over his bald head. "She's good. Bedrest is driving her crazy but her and the baby are both very healthy. As long as she stays put." He added. "She sends her love."

Tatiana had been Brett's waitress years before and ended up dating Kane, my best friend. They recently moved out of the city into the country and it felt like forever since I had seen them. But Skype and talking on the phone helped. Some.

"Brett, did you invite Kane?" I asked my husband when he stepped up beside us.

"I did. I know you've been missing him." Brett clapped a hand on Kane's shoulder.

"Did you show Evvie her office?" Kane asked.

"Not yet," Brett said. "You want to see your office?" he asked me.

"Yes!" I cried, clapping my hands together excitedly. I felt like a kid at Christmas.

He laughed and grabbed my hand. "We'll be back," he told my brothers while they entertained our children.

"Brett, this place is amazing. It must have taken you forever to get it just right." I craned my neck to see everything, all of the details of the club but it was so much to take in, it would take me hours to see it all.

"Well I had lots of help." He looked over my head and nodded.

I followed his gaze and saw Anna holding Patrick in her arms. She gave a little wave and blew me a kiss. I laughed and continued walking behind Brett to my office. My office. My very own space. I had the reading nook in our home but this…no one could disturb me if I just locked the door. No little hands pounding on the door, begging for my attention. No dark and brooding man demanding the attention of my body. As much as I loved it, I needed me time. Evvie time. God, this would be perfect. This would be…my eyes widened when I entered behind Brett into my office. It was…it was…"Brett."

"This is where you first kissed me." He allowed me to enter and closed the door. "This is where I first fingered your hot pussy," he breathed in my ear.

"It looks exactly like your office." It had the exact same desk, the dark leather couches, a minibar against the opposite wall and even a door leading into a bathroom behind the large office chair.

"It may be a little selfish, but I wanted you to think of me every time you walked into this room. Okay, so a lot selfish."

I laughed and turned in his arms. "This is amazing. Thank you. For everything."

"You are welcome." He pulled me to the couch, sitting me on his lap. "I wish I could have told you about this sooner to save you from the stress."

"No. This is perfect. I'm sorry for jumping to conclusions." I sighed happily and leaned against him. "This was the place where I first told you I loved you. I will always think of you every time that I'm here. Even if it didn't look like your club, I wouldn't be able to stop thinking about you anyways." I cupped his cheeks, straddling his lap. As soon as our pelvises touched, my heart sped up.

Brett inched his hands under my dress. "You still haven't learned not to wear panties," he said, kissing my neck and gripped the string of my thong. He pulled hard, igniting a gasp to escape my mouth. "I want you wet, constantly."

"I'm always wet for you."

Holding the fabric of my panties, his fingers brushed over my mound before he gave another tug. The soft material rubbed against my clit igniting a burn inside of me.

I moaned, only making him pull harder and faster.

"Kiss me. Like the first time." He lowered us to the couch, pushing his way between my thighs.

Cupping his nape, I brought his mouth down on mine. I licked my way between his lips, sucking and pulling at his tongue.

He growled and wrapped his free hand around my throat. "We're gonna make this quick. A tease for later." He nipped my bottom lip.

I whimpered, rocking my hips, hinting.

"We have the house to ourselves tonight and I'm going to fucking destroy your body."

***

A half an hour later and I was easing my racing heart, coming down from the high of the euphoria that had exploded through my body.

Brett continuously placed pecks on my neck, holding me tight against him, whispering every so often how much he loved me. How much he needed me and appreciated me.

I couldn't get enough. We had christened my office fast and hard, the sweet scent of our love wafting around us.

My throat was raw from the screaming he had forced out of me and if his promises about later rang true, I would have no voice the following day.

God, I loved the man holding me. I loved the life he had given me. And I loved him more for not giving up on us. He had thanked me time and time again for not giving up on him. In the beginning it was rough, issues with his mother, an ex, his stepfather…the list went on and on. But I loved him and only him. I was raised by stubborn men. There was no way that I was giving up that easily.

After almost losing me to cancer, Brett had become more protective but closed off. Like he was scared to love me too much for fear of losing me. He could never lose me. So many memories forced their way into my mind. Kids. Love. Us. Fighting. Making up. Although I had been mad at him only a couple of days ago, I now understood why he did what he did. Everything was for me. Everything was because of me.

In two days, it was our anniversary. Although I had forgotten about it, I would make up for it in ways that only he would understand. I would continue giving him all of me. I would continue giving him my submission and the passion that he craved. The control he needed. His rough grip on my body, even though he was only holding me, made me feel wanted and owned. *Claimed*.

Our love wrapped around us, stronger than ever. More powerful than ever before. We had our issues, but what marriage doesn't. We had our complications but the ropes of our love bound together, bringing us closer than ever.

My eyes became heavy, the soothing beat of his heart enveloping me in a dream like trance.

"I love you, Evvie MacLean. My wife. The mother of my children. My best friend. My *lover*." His words whispered over my skin.

"I love you deep," I whispered.

"I love you hard and I love you unconditionally." He kissed my cheek. "My one."

I let out a satisfied sigh, snuggling further into his side. "My only."

Six

"BRETT, THE weather is really coming down hard. We should pull over or something," I suggested, frowning as the rain beat down on our car.

"I can't see shit," he grumbled. "We never get rain like this."

"Yeah well, Mother Nature has been PMS-ing lately." It was the middle of the night. Brett had taken me out of town a week later to a remote bed and breakfast for our anniversary for a week so we could get away. It was romantic and one of the best weekends of my life but the drive was almost three hours. We had been driving slow because of the torrential rain but now I feared that we would get in an accident if we weren't careful. "Brett, please, can we stop. This is crazy."

"Evvie, I don't want to stop in the middle of nowhere. What if someone drove by and didn't see us?"

I sighed. "True. Wait! What's that?" I asked, pointing to something blocking the road.

"Shit," Brett mumbled. "It looks like a tree. I guess we have no choice but to stop."

"I see lights."

"Alright, we'll stop there and see if we can dry off or something as well until they get the road cleared."

As if on cue, a shiver ran down my back. We had to run to our car as we left the bed and breakfast and got caught in the rain. Our clothes were soaked and no matter how high we turned on the heater, I couldn't get warm.

We pulled into the parking lot and Brett shut off the car once reaching a free spot. The place was dark and dim but the lot was filled with vehicles.

"What is this place?" I asked, noting that there was no sign anywhere.

"Maybe someone lives here. I have no idea. I don't care either way. I'm getting you dry before you get sick." Before I could protest, he left the car and ran around to my door. He helped me out of the vehicle and I followed him to the entrance of the building.

"What if this is a private venue, Brett. Maybe we should just stay in the car until the rain stops."

"No," was all he said as he pushed open the front set of double doors.

The warmth of the inside wrapped around me, making me shiver uncontrollably. My teeth chattered.

Brett wrapped his arms around me, rubbing my arms, trying to warm me up. "We'll get warm and then leave."

"Excuse me? What are you doing here?"

We both looked at a large men approaching us.

"We got caught in the storm. We're sorry for intruding, we just need to get warm," Brett said, his voice firm but polite.

The man's brows furrowed. "This is a private club. You can't be in here."

"What's going on?" another man covered in tattoos asked, coming up beside the first guy.

"The front door wasn't locked like it should have been. They can't be in here."

"Aidan, the weather is shit."

The man named Aidan turned to us. "I'm sorry but you really can't be in here."

"We can at least let them sit in the lobby," the other man said. His piercing green eyes landed on me, warming.

"You can't stay here," the larger guy repeated. "It's an exclusive members-only night."

"It's raining out and there's a tree blocking the road," Brett explained. "Please. Even if you just let my wife sit in the lobby, I'll go wait in the car."

"We have to protect our members."

At that point, I saw a woman approach us. Her smooth tanned skin glowed in the moonlight. She was beautiful. She stepped up beside the man with the beautiful jade eyes and placed her hand in his.

"It's okay, Brett. We can wait in the car," I told Brett softly.

"No." He glared at Aidan.

The other woman stepped up between Aidan and Brett. "What's going on?"

"I thought we said for you to stay in the other room." Aidan's brows furrowed, his jaw clenching.

"We heard a bang and Liz asked me to check and make sure that you guys were okay." She turned to me. "If you come with me, I can get you dry clothes and put yours in a dryer."

My eyes widened. "Really? You would do that?"

"Of course," she said with a smile.

"Keely." The good looking guy with the green eyes leaned down to her ear. "You do know that you are going against what we told you."

A notable shiver ran through her. She nodded and whispered something softly to him.

He shook his head.

"Parker, they can't be in here. We have to protect our members," Aidan insisted.

Brett took a step towards him, going toe to toe with the man who was much larger than him. "Look. I see that you're married," he nodded towards the gold wedding band on Aidan's finger. "I can only assume that you would do anything for your spouse. Well, this is me, doing whatever I have to do for mine. Come with us if you have to but I'm not leaving until she gets dried off."

Keely pushed between the two of them. "Parker will be with us. Go check on Liz. She was scared," she told Aidan gently.

Aidan let out a huff. "Fine." And with that, he left the lobby and headed back to wherever this Liz was.

"I'm sorry about that. Aidan gets a little protective of his club." Parker cupped the back of Keely's neck and smiled down at her. "If it weren't for my wife, you would probably be headed back to your car by now."

"Thank you," Brett and I said in unison.

"It's no problem at all. What are your names?" Keely asked as they led us down a long hallway.

"I'm Evvie and this is my husband, Brett," I said, a shiver trembling through my body.

Brett wrapped his arm around his me. "If we were forced to go back to our car, I would warm you with my body."

I smiled up at him and kissed his cheek.

"Well it's nice to meet—"

"Wait," Parker stopped abruptly. "Are you Evvie and Brett MacLean?"

Brett and I looked at each other, small smiles spreading on our faces. "Yes. Why?"

"I knew it! You own *The Red Love* and several other clubs around the world." Parker grabbed a magazine from the side table by the wall. "See?"

Keely glanced at the picture of us standing before them in the tabloid. "Wow."

"This is embarrassing." I laughed once.

"Oh don't be embarrassed. Both of you are inspirational," she told me, grabbing the magazine from her husband.

"Really? You think so?" I smiled up at Brett, letting out a soft sigh.

"Yes," Parker answered. "It lets everyone know that you don't have to be born with a silver spoon in your mouth to become highly successful."

"Well I know that you are pretty successful yourself," Brett told him, running a hand through his short brown hair. He scratched the dark scruff on his strong jaw before pointing at Parker. "You own *Reed Industries*. But I had read somewhere several years ago that you died."

Keely cringed. "That is a whole other story."

I smacked my husband's arm. "What did I tell you about saying exactly what's on your mind?"

Brett grinned and kissed me hard on the mouth. "You've never complained before."

I scoffed. "I don't complain when you are open and honest with *me*. But you can't be that way with strangers. You have to get to know them first."

He shrugged and turned to Parker and Keely. "What are your names?"

"I'm Parker Reed, as you already guessed, and this is my wife, Keely," Parker replied.

"See?" Brett kissed my forehead. "Now we know them."

I rolled my eyes. "Forgive him. It's been a long day and we are finally kid-free thanks to my brothers."

Keely laughed. "We know that feeling."

"Oh? How many kids do you have?" I asked, gripping my husband's arm.

As we headed down the hall, we all talked about our children. How many we had, names, how old they were, and so on. It was nice to meet another couple with kids. I could only assume that my brothers would eventually have them but by the time they got their heads out of their asses, I would be old and grey.

"So, what kind of club is this?" I asked once we reached a room at the end of the hallway.

Parker and Keely glanced at each other.

"A private one," Keely answered, fingering the thin collar around her neck.

Brett raised an eyebrow. "Is this a club that we would be interested in?"

"Depends," Parker said, his eyes heating as he looked at his wife's collar.

I chewed my bottom lip. Interesting. "On what?"

Linking my arm in hers, Keely led me into the room that held costumes, extra clothes, and everything that I needed to get dried off. "It depends on if you have an open mind or not."

I laughed, my cheeks heating. "Um…well…"

A gasp resonated from the room making us all turn to the unexpected noise.

Brenda, a tall blonde, stood a few feet away from us, chewing her bottom lip and holding a black candle in her hands. The flame flickered, dancing in the air. "I am so sorry. I was waiting for the lights to turn back on before I left." Her gaze landed on Brett, her cheeks flushing a bright red.

I caught the look and giggled. "My husband has that effect on women," I whispered to Keely.

She joined in on my laughter. "So does mine. Women love his tattoos."

My grin widened. "Lucky we aren't the jealous types." Not anymore at least.

Keely nodded. "No doubt."

"Can you please grab a towel for me?" Brett asked Brenda.

"O-of c-course. I can do that. Sure thing." Her rambling was simply adorable as she stared wide-eyed at the man talking to her.

Keely shook her head and wrapped an arm around her shoulders. "Let's go before you drool all over yourself."

"I know he's taken but God, he's fucking hot," Brenda said, her voice taking on a dreamy singsong state. "Towel," Brenda said a moment later.

"Thank you." Keely took it from her and handed it to me as Brenda quickly left the room but not before she passed one last glance at Brett.

"I think someone has a crush on you," I teased, poking my husband playfully in the side.

He popped his collar, a smug smile forming on his face. "What can I say? I am irresistible and all."

"Wow. You sound just like Parker." Keely smiled, grabbing a change of clothes for me. "You can change in there." She nodded towards a small adjoining bathroom.

"So tell me about this place," Brett said as I stepped into the change room. "The secrecy has my curiosity peaked."

"Well…how about I show you instead? You got this?" I heard Parker ask Brett.

"Have fun. Your husband has gone with mine to check out the club," she told Evvie.

"Okay. What is this place anyways?" I asked, intrigued by the level of privacy this place had to offer. I didn't know what it was or what it consisted of but Brett and I was always looking for new experiences. I wondered if this place would appease our cravings.

"I guess putting it mildly, it's a fetish club."

For some reason, hearing those words, I wasn't surprised at all. Exclusive members only. No outsiders. It made sense. "What kind of fetish?" I asked, towel drying my hair as I stepped out of the small room.

"Um…well, anything really. Except for animals, this isn't that kind of club." She grimaced at the mere thought of it.

I laughed. "I guess you have to have a line that you can't cross."

"Exactly. I never thought you would be so cool about it."

"Why do you say that?" I asked, raising an eyebrow.

"Well," Keely shrugged. "I judged you too soon and I'm sorry for that. Usually it's the other way around but in this case, it was me."

I gave her a light hug. "I'm glad that we ran into this place. Brett and I were looking for…well…" My face went red hot. "Something exciting, to say the least."

At that moment, Brett and Parker came back into the room.

"Evvie," Brett said. "Come here."

My mouth parted and I walked up to my husband. "What—"

He covered my lips in a hard bruising kiss igniting a moan to escape me. He cupped the back of my neck. "We need this. I want to own you. I want to make you fly like I just saw."

"What do you mean?" I asked, breathless.

"I want to tie you up. God, Evvie. It makes me hard knowing the things I could do to you here." He kissed me again.

We both looked at Parker and Keely. "Where do we sign up?"

※ ※ ※ The End ※ ※ ※

About the Author

J.M. Walker is an Amazon bestselling author who loves all things books, pigs and lip gloss. She is happily married to the man who inspires all of her Heroes and continues to make her weak in the knees every single day.

"Above all, be the HEROINE of your own life..." ~ Nora Ephron

Website: http://www.aboutjmwalker.com/ - under construction
Facebook Fan Page: https://www.facebook.com/jm.walker.author
Reader Group: https://www.facebook.com/groups/752223284790825/
Twitter: https://twitter.com/jmwlkr
Instagram: https://www.instagram.com/jmwlkr/

CPSIA information can be obtained
at www.ICGtesting.com
Printed in the USA
BVHW031814240320
575860BV00001B/37

9 781365 806957